Hi! I'm Darcy J. Doyle, Daring Detective,

but you can call me D.J. The only thing better than reading a good mystery is solving one. When it looked like our fifth grade play might be canceled and Max might lose his big chance to be a star, I had to do something about it. Let me tell you about The Case of the Angry Actress.

Books in the Darcy J. Doyle,

Daring Detective series:

The Case of the Angry Actress
The Case of the Bashful Bully
The Case of the Choosey Cheater
The Case of the Creepy Campout
The Case of the Giggling Ghost
The Case of the Missing Max
The Case of the Mixed-Up Monsters
The Case of the Pampered Poodle

The Case of the Angry Actress

Linda Lee Maifair

ZondervanPublishingHouse
Grand Rapids, Michigan

A Division of HarperCollins*Publishers*

The Case of the Angry Actress

Request for information should be addressed to:
Zondervan Publishing House
Grand Rapids, Michigan 49530

ISBN 0-310-43301-0

Edited by Dave Lambert
Interior design by Rachel Hostetter
Illustrations by Tim Davis
Cover design by Anne Huizenga

Printed in the United States of America

94 95 96 97 98 99 / ❖ OP / 10 9 8 7 6 5 4 3 2 1

In memory of my grandparents,
Elmer and Nettie Conaway

CHAPTER 1

I'm Darcy J. Doyle. Some of my friends call me Darcy. Some just call me D.J. If I keep on solving important cases, pretty soon everyone will be calling me Darcy J. Doyle, Daring Detective. It's only a matter of time.

My last big case started the day our language arts teacher, Miss Woodson, called a special meeting of the whole fifth grade.

"This year's fifth-grade play will be *The Princess and the Dragon,*" Miss Woodson announced. Then she read us the story.

We loved it. It had everything — a king, knights, a scary dragon, and lots of laughs. And best of all, in the end it isn't the knights who save the kingdom from the dragon. It's a couple of kids, Princess Rosabella and her friend Chadrick, along with her trusty dog, Thor. They make *friends* with the dragon, so that it doesn't want to destroy things any more. Neat.

"We'll need some knights," Miss Woodson said.

About twenty kids waved their hands in the air, but Miss Woodson motioned for the kids to put down their hands. "You can sign up for parts later this afternoon," she said. "Besides the knights, we'll need a king, a court jester, some ladies of the court, a couple of people to be our dragon — "

A whole bunch of hands went up for that, too.

Miss Woodson waved the hands down. "And of course, we'll need a Princess Rosabella and a Chadrick." She smiled again. "I'll post the sign-up sheets in the back of my room this afternoon. We'll have auditions on Wednesday."

All through lunch and recess, the whole fifth grade talked about one thing only: which parts we wanted in the play.

"I'm going to try to be a knight," Nick said. "I could make some really cool armor out of cardboard and aluminum foil."

Mandy wanted to be one of the ladies and dress up in a long, fancy gown.

"I want to be a dragon and breathe smoke!" Sammy Lee yelled.

"Yeah, me too!" Enrico and Josh both said at the same time.

"We can all *three* fit into a dragon costume — we can make a *big* dragon," Enrico said. The three of them lined up, one behind the other, and stomped across the cafeteria chasing fourth graders and making scary dragon sounds. Everybody except Mrs. Allen, the cafeteria monitor, thought it was hilarious.

"You should try out for the part of Rosabella," Mandy told me. "You'd be good at it."

"*Me*?" I shook my head. I remembered the time I had a big part in our church Christmas program. I took one look at the audience and forgot what I was supposed to say. It was embarrassing. "I get too nervous," I said.

Mandy couldn't believe it. "Darcy Doyle, *Daring* Detective, gets nervous?" she said.

Being daring in the middle of a big case was one thing. Being daring on a stage in front of a roomful of parents was something else. "I'd rather face a *real* dragon," I said. "I'll volunteer to help with props or something."

One of the girls in my class, Shari Meyers, overheard me. "*Props*!" she said. The way she wrinkled up her nose, you'd have thought I was going to volunteer to scrub out the garbage barrels in the school cafeteria. "You'd settle for a *little* job like that?"

I hate it when people talk to me like that. "*Somebody's* got to do it," I said. "And besides, Pastor Jordan — that's our minister at church — is always telling us that *all* jobs are important. It's not what you do but how you do it that counts."

Shari made another garbage-barrel face. "Well, props may be okay for *you*," she said. "But *I* want a part in the play — a *big* part! I'm going to try out for Princess Rosabella."

I wasn't a bit surprised when I saw Shari's name on top of the "Princess Rosabella" sign-up list that afternoon. And she wasn't alone — six girls wanted to try out for the part: Shari,

Cheryl Klein, Latonya Shurburne, Rebecca Covington, Emily Washington, and Sondra Orkowski.

The play assignments were announced on Thursday morning. Rebecca Covington got the part of Princess Rosabella. Leon got the part of Chadrick. And Miss Woodson put me in charge of the Props Committee.

She even asked me if my faithful bloodhound, Max, could do the part of Thor. "All he'd have to do is follow Rebecca and Leon across the stage a few times," she said. "But if you don't think he could handle it, it's okay. We'll just cut the dog out of the story."

This was Max's big chance! If I gave Rebecca and Leon a pocketful of dog biscuits, Max would follow them anywhere. "Don't worry, Miss Woodson," I told her. "Max is very trustworthy."

I was really sort of pleased about the way it had turned out. Max was going to be a star. And Shari Meyers was going to be the court jester, one of the *littlest* roles in the play.

"Serves her right," I told Mandy on the way home from school that afternoon.

CHAPTER 2

We had our first play rehearsal on Monday afternoon.

Miss Woodson passed out copies of the script. The actors read through their parts out loud while Andy Malone, the head of the Sound Effects Committee, made a list of all the music and noises we'd be needing. Debbie Bernstein, the head of the Costume Committee, made a list of costume ideas.

I kept a list of props. I couldn't wait to start hunting for the things on my list: a dozen goblets and plates, two oversized chairs, some old-fashioned candlesticks, ten shields and swords, a pouch of gold, a chest of jewels, something to make the dragon smoke, and a whole bunch of other stuff.

Mandy and I looked over the list on the way home from school. "This will be fun," I said. "Sort of like a mystery."

Mandy laughed. *"Everything's* a mystery to you, D.J."

She was right. I smiled. "What's *really* a mystery to me is why Miss Woodson is keeping Shari Meyers as the jester. I thought jesters were supposed to *smile* and make people happy."

Shari had spent the whole rehearsal pouting and scowling and glaring at Rebecca Covington. Shari's part in the play was pretty small — she had two jokes to tell. They were corny, but funny. But the way Shari read them, you'd have thought she was reading somebody's funeral notice.

Mandy nodded. "I guess she's still mad because Rebecca is Princess Rosabella."

"Well," I said, "I hope she gets over it before the performance. Besides, Rebecca's really good as the princess."

Mandy agreed. "She read her part better than anybody."

We did our homework together at my house. Then we got ready to go to some of the neighbors to ask if they could loan us any of the stuff on the props list. I hooked Max's leash onto his collar to take him along.

"You sure that's a good idea?" Mandy asked.

"Why not?" I said. "You know what a big help good old Max can be."

"Like the way he helped us pitch the tent in the backyard last weekend?" Mandy reminded me.

"Dad says we needed a new tent anyway." I waved Mandy out the door before she could remind me of anything else.

Mrs. Anderson had two big old chairs in her attic. Covered with red cloth, they would make great thrones. "You're welcome to use them for the play," Mrs. Anderson said, "if you'll donate them to the mission afterward."

I told her Dad would be glad to take them to the mission. I also promised to come back the next afternoon and fill in the hole Max had dug under her hedges while the rest of us were up in the attic looking at the chairs.

Mrs. Billings had a bunch of plastic throw-away wine glasses left over from her daughter's wedding reception. Sprayed with paint, they would look like silver goblets. She gave us the whole box.

I thanked her and promised I'd bring her a new bag of marshmallows to replace the ones

Max had eaten while the rest of us were down in the cellar looking for the glasses.

Miss Witherspoon let our church's women's organization store their rummage-sale collections in her garage. She let us root around in the bags and boxes. We found a great wooden jewelry box and a lot of glittery costume jewelry to put in it.

When we came out of the garage, we found Max standing half in and half out of Mrs. Witherspoon's overturned garbage can.

Mandy laughed. "Some help he's been!" she said.

I gave her one of my looks as I tugged at Max's leash and yanked him backward, out of the can. He came out with spaghetti sauce on his nose and a well-licked aluminum pie plate in his mouth.

He dropped the pie plate at my feet. "Thanks, Max," I said.

Mandy wrinkled her nose at me. "What are you thanking *him* for? All he's done is made another mess for you to clean up."

"Good old Max was *not* making a mess," I explained. I picked up the pie plate. "He went to all this trouble just to show me what we could use for plates." I patted him on the head. "Isn't that right, boy?"

Max licked at the red splotches around his mouth. "Woof! Woof!" he said.

When we got home, I checked off the things we'd found on my props list. I couldn't wait for my Props Committee to meet after lunch the next day. "They'll be surprised at how well we've done," I told Mandy.

The committee was surprised. But not nearly as surprised as I was when I walked into the library for the meeting. Our committee had another member.

"I thought getting props wasn't a big enough job for you," I told Shari Meyers.

She shrugged. "I decided I might as well help out since my part is so — " She couldn't say it.

I could have finished it for her. So *small*. But I didn't.

"Unless you don't want me," Shari said.

If she was willing, I couldn't say no. I gave her the box of plastic glasses and the can of silver spray paint Dad had donated. "We can always use more help," I said.

CHAPTER 3

On Friday afternoon, Miss Woodson told the cast to work on memorizing their parts over the weekend.

"We only have three weeks before the play," she said. She smiled brightly. "Last year more than three hundred people came to our fifth-grade play. Most of your parents, grandparents, and brothers and sisters will be there."

I could imagine my feet turning to stone and my stomach turning to cold mush in front of three hundred parents, grandparents, and brothers and sisters. I was glad I hadn't tried out for a part.

"Aren't you nervous?" I asked Rebecca Covington. As Princess Rosabella, she had more lines to learn than anyone else.

"Me?" she said. Her face was pale. And she sort of chewed at her lower lip. "Uh, no. Of course not."

I decided it might not be such a good idea to tell her how nervous she *looked*. "You'll be great," I said.

Our first onstage rehearsal was Monday morning. Those who knew their lines were supposed to say them without reading them. And the kids started acting out the parts for the first time. It didn't go very well.

First, the king and queen and princess raised their goblets to salute the brave knights who were going off to fight the dragon. The fruit punch in Princess Rosabella's glass dribbled out all over her.

"There's a *hole* in my cup!" Rebecca sputtered. She wiped the dripping red punch off her chin with the back of her hand. Then she held the goblet up to the light. "There's a *whole bunch* of holes!"

Miss Woodson sent the princess to the restroom to wash her face. While Rebecca was gone, Miss Woodson inspected the glass herself. She showed it to me. "She's right, Darcy. Look at this."

I held up the glass and squinted at the row of ragged, round holes punched in the side, near the rim. "I don't know how this happened, Miss Woodson," I said. I had checked the goblets myself, after Shari finished painting them. "Those holes weren't in there this morning."

Miss Woodson looked around at the cast and crew. "I hope this isn't somebody's idea of a joke," she said.

Rebecca came back, and the rehearsal went on. Princess Rosabella and Chadrick were approaching the dragon's cave. "Come out, dragon!" Princess Rosabella said, bravely.

It was the first line she'd remembered right all morning.

She and Chadrick pulled their cardboard swords from their cardboard sheaths. Chadrick's sword came right out, the way it was supposed to. Princess Rosabella's sword didn't budge.

Rebecca pulled and tugged. Finally, she grabbed the hilt of the sword with both hands and gave it a mighty heave. The hilt of the sword came off in her hand. The rest of the sword stayed in the sheath. She stood there with her mouth wide open and the sword hilt in her hand. She looked ridiculous.

Miss Woodson shushed the kids' laughter and went over to see what was wrong. "It was stuck!" Rebecca told her. "It wouldn't come out!"

I couldn't believe it. First the goblet and now the sword. "We checked *all* of the swords after we finished making them, Miss Woodson," I said. My Props Committee had tried out every sword and sheath. "They all worked fine."

Miss Woodson tried to pull the remains of the sword out of the sheath herself. "It's as if something's holding — " she started to say.

She turned the sheath around and looked at the bottom. Then she looked at the fifth graders standing all around. She did not look happy. "This sheath has been stapled to the sword so it won't come out."

That was the end of rehearsal. Instead of finishing the play, Miss Woodson gave us a talk about practical jokes and how they weren't very funny. "I'd hate to have to cancel the play," she warned us.

The other kids were really disappointed that the play might be called off. But I wasn't disappointed — I was *angry*. Someone had tampered with the props. And the props were *my* responsibility.

"I'd like to know who our practical joker is," Mandy said when we went to the cloakroom to get our jackets and book bags.

"I have an idea," I told her.

"You do?"

It hadn't been very hard for my daring detective mind to figure out. I slipped on my jacket and nodded. "Who did both things happen to?"

"Rebecca Covington," Mandy said.

I nodded again. "And who was really mad that Rebecca got the part of Princess Rosabella?"

Mandy gasped. "You think Shari Meyers did it?"

"Who else would want to make Rebecca look silly and ruin the whole play?" I snapped my jacket and took my book bag off the hook. Then I turned around and found myself face-to-face with Rebecca Covington.

"I, uh — " I didn't know how to apologize for saying she'd looked silly.

"I'll pay you if you can prove it," she said.

"Huh?"

"If you prove that Shari is behind the practical jokes, I'll pay you. You're a detective, aren't you?"

"Sure she is," Mandy told Rebecca. "She's Darcy J. Doyle, Daring Detective. She can solve any mystery."

"And you'll take my case?" Rebecca asked me.

"Sure she will," Mandy said again.

I thought of how Shari Meyers had made Rebecca Covington look silly. I thought of how she had made my Props Committee look bad.

I thought of how she must have volunteered for the committee just to get her hands on the props for her practical jokes. I thought of how she might ruin the play for the whole fifth grade.

I gave Rebecca Covington my most confident Daring Detective smile. "It'll be a pleasure," I said.

CHAPTER 4

Max and I were in the kitchen having milk and cookies when my pesty brother Allen got home from soccer practice.

He took one look at my notebook and groaned. "*Now* what's the great detective working on?" he said.

I ignored him, but he didn't go away. He came and stood behind me, reading my notes over my shoulder:

Shari wanted part. Didn't get it.

Didn't want to do props. Then volunteered for Props Committee.

Painted the goblets. Goblet had holes punched in the side.

Helped put the swords in the sheaths. Sheath stapled to sword.

Shari only person with motive.

"What's a *motive*?" Allen asked.

It's hard to ignore someone who's leaning on your back, breathing stale barbeque-potato-chip breath into your face.

I moved my chair a few inches away from him. "A motive is a reason for doing something. Like when you glued together the pages of my new mystery book. That gave me a motive for bopping you."

Allen grinned. "And *that*," he said, "gave Dad a motive for sending you to your room without dessert."

I was sorry I'd brought it up. "Somebody's been pulling practical jokes on Rebecca Covington at play practice. Shari Meyers is the only one with a motive. She wanted the part herself."

Allen sat down and helped himself to one of my cookies. "Was Shari the only one who wanted the part?" He stuffed the whole cookie in his mouth.

Max grumbled at him. Good old Max. He hated to see anyone question the conclusions of Darcy J. Doyle, Daring Detective. I broke a cookie in two and gave half to Max. He thumped his thanks with his tail against the floor.

"Shari was the only one who was mad enough to do something about it," I told Allen.

He took my notebook and read my clues again. He popped another cookie in his mouth and talked around it. It was disgusting. "Is she the only one who worked on the swords and goblets?"

Max grumbled again. I patted him on the head and rewarded him with another cookie. "No, she wasn't the *only* one," I told Allen, annoyed. "The whole Props Committee handled the glasses and swords." A bunch of the actors had, too.

"Then how do you know — "

I didn't want to hear any more. I picked up my notebook and a handful of cookies and left the room. Max went with me. Good old Max. Always ready to stick up for me.

Allen blabbed about my new case at dinner — between the chicken and dumplings and the strawberry fluff.

"Are you *sure* it's Shari Meyers?" Mom asked.

"Sounds like a lot of kids had access to those props," Dad reminded me.

They sounded like Allen. They should have been congratulating me for solving the case so quickly instead of doubting me. It made me angry. *I'll show them!* I thought.

I was so upset I turned down dessert and excused myself from the table. I went straight to my room to figure out how to prove that Shari Meyers was the culprit and that Darcy J. Doyle had been right all along.

But it was hard to concentrate on my detective work. All I could think of was strawberry fluff.

CHAPTER 5

I put my plan into action the very next day.

At lunch, I found Shari Meyers sitting at the cafeteria table staring at a half-eaten plate of Noodle Surprise.

"I need your help, Shari," I said.

She shoved her platter away. "Sure," she said. "What do you want me to do?"

"Mom's bringing my dog, Max, over after recess this afternoon so he can practice his part in the play. I'll be busy with him, so I won't be able to work backstage." Usually, during rehearsal, I stood backstage with a list of the props and made sure everything got on stage at the right time. "Could you do that for me?"

"You want *me* to do it?" Shari put a hand on her stomach and gave me a queasy sort of smile.

Probably her guilty conscience bothering her, I thought. "Absolutely," I said.

Feeling pretty smug about the trap I was setting, I left Shari in the cafeteria. Instead of going out to recess, I went to the stage in the gym to make sure everything was ready for rehearsal. Then I went out to the front of the school just in time to meet Mom and Max.

"If there's a problem, just call," Mom told me. "I'll come and get him."

I took Max's leash and pulled him from the station wagon. "When has Max ever been a problem?" I asked.

Mom opened and closed her mouth, as if she had started to say something and then changed her mind. "I'll be home all afternoon," she said.

I waved good-bye to my mother and led Max into the school. I took him straight to the gym. The cast and crew had gotten there ahead of me. "All set?" Miss Woodson asked me.

I held up the bag of doggie treats Mom had brought with her. "Max is ready — aren't you, boy?"

Max woofed loudly. I gave him one of the doggie treats. "Just tell me what you need him to do," I told Miss Woodson.

She smiled doubtfully at Max. "Well, maybe we should walk him through it a couple of times. With the leash. Then we'll take it from there."

So we walked through the scene where Princess Rosabella and Chadrick and Thor walked up to the dragon's cave. Rebecca and Leon walked side by side in front. Max and I followed behind. Max thought it was some sort of game. He wagged his tail the whole way.

"Come out, dragon!" Princess Rosabella said.

She pulled her sword. Chadrick pulled his. Both swords worked the way they were supposed to.

"Speak, Max!" I said. I held out a doggie treat.

"Woof, woof!" he said loudly.

I gave him the treat. Miss Woodson and all the kids applauded.

We walked through it again. Then I let Max get a whiff of a liver doggie treat and passed the treat to Leon. I unhooked Max's leash. Rosabella and Chadrick walked across the stage. Max followed them.

"Come out, dragon!" the princess said.

She and Chadrick pulled their swords. Holding the liver treat in his other hand, Leon waved it behind his back at Max. "Woof, woof!" Max said.

Miss Woodson smiled a relieved sort of smile. "Perfect!" she said.

Max's other scenes went just as well. Miss Woodson even said he was a "natural-born actor." I was feeling really good as I sat next to him watching the kids practice the rest of the play. Except for Rebecca Covington mixing up her lines, there wasn't a single problem — until they got to the very last scene.

By that time, the dragon had proven his friendship by saving the king and queen. The king named him Chief Protector of the kingdom. Princess Rosabella was to award medals to the dragon, Chadrick, and Thor. First, Rebecca draped a red ribbon around Leon's neck. Then she tied one to Thor's collar. Then she climbed up on a stool to reach the dragon.

The dragon thumped forward. Inside the dragon costume, of course, were Josh and Enrico and Sammy Lee. Josh was in the front. He tilted the big cardboard dragon head forward. The princess reached up to drape the chain of the medallion around his neck.

Crash! The stool went one way and, still holding onto the chain, Rebecca went the other, pulling the dragon's head after her. Rebecca landed on the floor. The dragon's head landed on top of her.

This time, nobody thought it was funny. Miss Woodson ran over to Rebecca. "Are you all right?" she asked. "What happened?"

Rebecca wiped back her tears. "My ankle hurts," she said. "The stool. It fell apart."

Miss Woodson sent Leon to get the school nurse to look at Rebecca's ankle. Then she

picked up the stool. I'd never seen her look so disappointed — or angry. "This leg was loosened on purpose," she said.

Rebecca started to cry. "I . . . I don't want . . . to be the princess . . . anymore," she sobbed. "I can't . . . be in . . . the play."

Miss Woodson handed her a tissue. "There isn't going to be any play, Rebecca," she said. She looked at the rest of us. "Not unless the person responsible for these . . . these *jokes* . . . comes forward and confesses."

I looked around for Shari Meyers. The least she could do was confess so that the play wouldn't have to be cancelled. But she didn't even come out from behind the stage curtains. I didn't see her anywhere.

Rebecca was taken to the nurse's office to put an ice pack on her ankle. Miss Woodson sent the rest of the fifth grade back to their classrooms. Then she walked over to Max and me.

"You were really great, Max," she said, patting him on the head. "You'd better call and have your mother come and get him, Darcy."

I decided it was time for the Daring Detective to tell what she knew. "Miss Woodson, you don't have to cancel the play. I know who's been doing all these things to Rebecca."

Miss Woodson looked surprised. "You do?"

I nodded. "It's Shari, Miss Woodson."

"Shari Meyers?" Miss Woodson asked.

"Yes," I said. "She was mad because she didn't get the part. She volunteered for the Props Committee, so she worked with those goblets and swords. And I . . ." I hesitated.

"And you what?" Miss Woodson asked.

"I'm sorry, Miss Woodson. I should have told you about Shari before. Then Rebecca wouldn't have gotten hurt. But I wanted to prove that it was Shari. So I checked all the props at recess, and I asked Shari to work backstage for me this afternoon. That way, if anything happened, I'd know for sure that Shari did it. All I had to do was put two and two together. It all adds up," I said.

Miss Woodson put a hand on my shoulder. "You're a terrific detective, Darcy," she said. "But math has never been your best subject."

I didn't understand. "What?"

"I'm afraid you put two and two together and came up with five," Miss Woodson said. "If you checked that stool right before practice, then Shari couldn't have been responsible."

I *had* checked the stool, along with all the other props. "Why not?" I asked.

"Because Shari Meyers never got to the gym this afternoon. She wasn't even here for recess.

She got sick to her stomach at lunch. The nurse sent her home."

Shari Meyers went home sick at lunch? She hadn't been backstage at all?

"I don't feel so well myself," I told Miss Woodson. And it wasn't from the Noodle Surprise.

Everybody who had heard my clues — Mom, Dad, even my brother Allen! — had tried to tell me. And everybody had been right — except me.

CHAPTER 6

I was lying on my bed, staring at my notebook, when Allen invited himself into my room. He stood next to my bed, chomping on an apple.

"Whatcha doing?" he asked.

I was not in a good mood. "Sleeping," I said. "Go away."

He waved his apple at my notebook. "Thought you had your big case all solved," he said. "Thought you were sure it was Shari Meyers."

"A good detective explores all the possibilities before making an accusation," I told him.

Allen wrinkled his nose at me. "Huh?"

"I have to be sure before I say somebody did it," I explained. "Sort of like what Pastor Jordan said last Sunday. About not judging people too quickly." I wished I had remembered that *before* I told Miss Woodson about Shari.

"Oh." Allen lost interest in the conversation. He took his apple on down the hall to his bedroom.

I sighed at the lists I had made in my notebook. All the girls who had wanted the part of Princess Rosabella. All the kids on the Props Committee. All the people who could have been backstage before the final scene of the play.

I had plenty of suspects now. But which of them had wanted Rebecca out of the play? Who wanted the play to be cancelled?

I had no idea. I tossed the notebook on the bed and went downstairs to use the telephone. I was just looking up Shari Meyers' number when Max came running through the kitchen growling and shaking something in his teeth. It was long and red and soggy and tattered. The ribbon Rebecca Covington had tied around his neck at practice. He shook it a few more times and dropped it on the floor at my feet.

"I don't have time to play now, Max," I told him. I picked up the ribbon and tossed it to him. He caught it between his teeth and bounded off toward the living room with it dragging from his mouth.

I called Shari to see how she was feeling. It's too bad *confessing* to mistakes is so much

harder than *making* them. I couldn't quite get out an apology for thinking she'd been the one who loosened the leg of the stool. It made me feel sort of guilty when she thanked me for calling.

Then I called Rebecca Covington. Her mother answered the phone. "Rebecca isn't here right now, Darcy," she said. "She's out riding her bike."

I was glad to hear that her ankle was better. "I guess she's really disappointed," I told Mrs. Covington.

"Disappointed?" she said.

"About the play being cancelled," I explained. "I know how much she was looking forward to playing Princess Rosabella."

Mrs. Covington laughed. "Rebecca's hardly disappointed, Darcy. She wanted to quit the play a week ago, when she found out how many people were going to be there and how hard it would be to memorize her lines."

About the same time I said good-bye to Mrs. Covington, Max came barreling back into the kitchen. He gave the ribbon a couple of furious shakes, then spit it out in a soggy heap at my feet. He growled and grumbled at it and wagged his tail.

I held the ribbon up by one of its shredded ends. "Woof! Woof!" Max said. "Woof! Woof!"

I patted him on the head. Max always knew a clue when he saw one. "You had this case figured out before I did, boy," I said.

He snatched the ribbon from my hand and took off toward the stairs, up to my bedroom. I ran after him. Good old Max. He knew I'd be needing my notebook. And he was always anxious to wrap up another big case.

CHAPTER 7

Rebecca Covington limped into homeroom the next morning. When she limped off with the rest of the class to go to the library, I stayed behind to talk to Miss Woodson.

"I did the math problem over, Miss Woodson," I said.

She tilted her head. "What problem was that, Darcy?"

"You know. Two plus two," I said. "This time I'm sure I got four."

She motioned me to the chair beside her desk. "Tell me about it," she said.

So I did. And when I was finished, I said, "I'm sure this time, Miss Woodson."

She sat back in her chair and raised one eyebrow at me. "You were sure the last time, too," she reminded me.

I nodded. "But this time," I said, "I think I have a way to prove it." I told her my plan.

When the class came back from the library, Miss Woodson gave them some vocabulary words to write into sentences. "Darcy," Miss Woodson said to me, "would you help Rebecca go down to the nurse's office, please? I don't like the way she's limping. I want Mrs. Jacobson to look at it again."

Rebecca's face turned pale. "It's not that bad, Miss Woodson. Really. We don't have to bother Mrs. Jacobson."

Miss Woodson shook her head. "It's no bother, Rebecca. That's her job. Besides, if she says it's healing okay, you might be able to be in the play after all."

Rebecca leaned on my shoulder and limped down the hall to the nurse's office. Mrs. Jacobson helped Rebecca to a chair and knelt down in front of her. "Let's take another look at that ankle," she said.

"It still hurts to walk on it." Rebecca held out her left foot. "I don't think I can be in — "

But Mrs. Jacobson gave her a funny look and interrupted her. "That's not the ankle you showed me yesterday, Rebecca."

Rebecca glanced down at her foot, as if she thought she might have made a mistake. "Yes, it is, Mrs. Jacobson."

Mrs. Jacobson shook her head slowly. "It was your *right* foot yesterday."

Rebecca looked scared. "I should know which ankle it was!" she said. But she stared at first one foot, then the other, as if she wasn't all that sure any more.

"Mrs. Jacobson's right, Rebecca," Miss Woodson said. "It *was* your other foot yesterday. How can that be?"

Rebecca tried to come up with an explanation. "Uh, well . . . I must have . . . Maybe it . . . When I walked to . . ." She gave up. "I don't know!" she wailed.

Miss Woodson put a hand on her shoulder. "Your ankle isn't hurt, is it, Rebecca? Neither ankle is hurt, is it?"

Rebecca's eyes filled with tears.

"You loosened the leg on that stool yourself, didn't you?" Miss Woodson went on.

Rebecca wiped the tears from her cheek. "Why — why would I want to do that?"

"So you wouldn't have to be in the play," I said. "So you'd have a good reason to quit."

Rebecca didn't say anything.

"Cheryl Klein set the table for the banquet scene," I went on. "She says there weren't any holes in the cup then. You were the only one who touched it after that. All the serving girl did was pour the punch into the goblet."

"I — I *didn't,*" Rebecca protested. She didn't sound very convincing. "It was Shari. You know that."

This time I had done my detective work right. "Shari couldn't have loosened the leg on the stool, Rebecca. She wasn't here."

"She — she gave me the sword sheath to put on, though," Rebecca said.

I nodded. "I know. She even helped you to hook it around your waist. But then you went to the rest room, before you went on stage. That's when you stapled the sheath and sword together, isn't it?"

"I can understand how you felt, Rebecca," Miss Woodson told her. "You were having a bad case of stage fright. You were having trouble memorizing your lines. You were too embarrassed to ask me to take you out of the play. I'm not angry at you. But now I need you to tell me the truth."

I knew how Rebecca felt. Making mistakes was easy. Confessing them was hard. I smiled. "Max is going to be real disappointed if the play is cancelled," I said.

Rebecca wiped her eyes again. "I'm sorry, Miss Woodson," she said. "Really I am."

CHAPTER 8

When the fifth grade presented "The Princess and the Dragon," Shari Meyers did a great job as Princess Rosabella. All the props worked the way they were supposed to — even the dry-ice smoke for the dragon.

And Max was the star of the show. He even got his picture in the local paper. Of course, he didn't exactly follow the script.

In the banquet scene, he put his front paws on the table. He slurped the fruit punch out of the king's goblet and kissed the queen on the nose. Then he chased one of the serving girls and her platter full of cakes off the stage. The audience applauded.

The princess, Chadrick, and Thor went off to meet the dragon. Max followed Leon across the stage. The dragon came out, smoking and stomping and growling. The brave and trusty Thor took one look at the smoke, which he hadn't seen before, and let out a howl. Then, with his tail between his legs, he tried to hide behind the big cardboard trees of the "forest" near the cave.

Princess Rosabella and Chadrick just stood there and watched, mouths hanging open, as trees tumbled in all directions. Trees crashed to the stage. They tumbled off the stage. And Thor ran off toward the curtain, howling all the way. The audience loved it.

In the final scene, when the dragon got his medal, Thor attacked the dragon's long, green tail. He jumped on it. Chewed on it. Growled

Bayside Elementary Play a Hit! Canine Comedian Steals Show

Bayside — The fifth grade play at Bayside Elementary School took an unexpected twist during Friday night's performance. Max, the pet dog of student Darcy Doyle, kept the audience laughing all night with a series of funny miscues. Miss Janice Woodson, who directed the play, said that the script at it. Shook it like an old rag. He finally tore off the end of the tail while the whole cast finished the play trying to pretend that nothing out of the ordinary was going on.

Max still had the tip of the tail in his mouth when the cast came out for their bow at the end of the play. He got the biggest round of applause from the audience, too.

When the play was over, I congratulated Shari Meyers on how well she had done as Princess Rosabella. I told Rebecca she'd done a good job as the jester, too.

The next day, I bought an extra copy of the newspaper. I cut out the picture of Max. I taped it — next to the piece of tattered red ribbon — in my scrapbook of important cases solved by Darcy J. Doyle, Daring Detective.

Catch Up on All of Darcy's Cases!

The Case of the Mixed-Up Monsters

Book 1 $2.99 0-310-57921-X

Somebody has been making a mess in the neighborhood, and everybody thinks it's Darcy's pesky little brother. Join Darcy as she gets to the truth.

The Case of the Choosey Cheater

Book 2 $2.99 0-310-57901-5

The big game is coming, and somebody is stealing homework. Darcy thinks the two are linked, but she doesn't have much time to solve the mystery.

The Case of the Giggling Ghost

Book 3 $2.99 0-310-57911-2

Is Mrs. Pendleton's house really haunted? What about all those noises? It's up to Darcy to solve the mystery.

The Case of the Pampered Poodle

Book 4 $2.99 0-310-57891-4

Fifi, the prize-winning poodle, has disappeared—right before the pet show. It takes faithful Max and a special kind of courage for Darcy to solve this case.

The Case of the Creepy Campout

Book 5 $2.99 0-310-43271-5

When things keep going wrong on the youth group campout, everybody thinks Tricia is causing the problems. It's Darcy's job to find out the truth.

The Case of the Bashful Bully

Book 6 $2.99 0-310-43281-2

Nobody can figure out the new boy. Nice one minute, fighting the next. What's going on? It's a race between Darcy and the snoopy school reporter to find out.

The Case of the Angry Actress

Book 7 $2.99 0-310-43301-0

Somebody's rude "practical jokes" could stop the school play. Who is the culprit? It's up to Darcy to find an answer before the play is canceled.

The Case of the Missing Max

Book 8 $2.99 0-310-43311-8

Vacation with Grandma and Grandpa was supposed to be fun, but instead Darcy is frantic. Her faithful dog, Max, has disappeared!